The Wanderer

and the

Strange Loop

The Wanderer

and the
Strange Loop

S.F. Augsburger

Achronos Media

ISBN-10: 0-692-93895-8
ISBN-13: 978-0-692-93895-9

10 9 8 7 6 5 4 3 2 1

Table of Contents

Listen!

Perplexed, he knelt in the damp debris next to the rock. No simple geological fracture produced its sheer faces, for there were signs of artistic effort in its smooth facets and sharp edges. He brushed away the leaves and dirt to reveal an inscription that read,

Listen!
Is is not and IsNot is
Many are one
One is many
Seek to understand!

Time seemed to slow down as he stood there, fixated on the rock and its message. *Was it intended for him?* He shook his head, surfacing. *Surely not!* With deliberate effort, he tried to avoid its challenge. *It could be for anyone! Or everyone! What has it to do with my mission? After all, my mission is noble.* Trivial riddles would only distract him from his purpose.

Turning from the rock, he continued down the path through the woods. The sun was in front of him and to the left, casting lengthy shadows from the trees. The leaves, past their prime, were loosing their grip on the trees, and quickly covering the path. Autumn was coming to a close. He hoped his mission would be complete before winter set in. Surely, it would only take a week or so.

Weary as he was, he found himself walking carefully, but with some haste in the approaching dusk. He wanted to find a place to rest before nightfall. The journey felt as though it had taken forever; and yet, it strangely seemed as though he was moving outside of time. His purpose was, after all, timeless.

The woods cleared and the path began to wander through a meadow of tall grass. Below, in the valley to the west, he could see the village. He had been told of its location and quaint nature. Many a traveler returned again and again, once introduced to its strange aura.

At the village's entrance, an elderly man was leading sheep to their stalls for the night. The Elder was hunched over, face to the ground. "Pardon me," he said to the Elder. "Would you know where I could stay for the night?"

The old man replied without lifting his head, "Listen Inn."

"OK," he said, "I am listening."

"No," said the gentleman, "Listen Inn! You will want to stay at Listen Inn."

"Oh, I am sorry, sir. I thought you meant . . ."

"Not to worry, young man. It's not the first time I have been misunderstood. It happens again and again."

"Where can I find Listen Inn?"

"Go straight into town," said the Elder, directing him to follow the main roadway into the center of the village where the inn had been welcoming travelers for centuries.

Entering the inn, he rang the bell on the front desk. "Can I help you?" called the innkeeper, as she entered the foyer.

"Uh, yes, do you have a vacancy?"

"Allesa Horen's the name, since you asked. Welcome to Listen Inn."

"I'm sorry. Nice to meet you, Ms. Horen. I'm Fritz Streuner."

"Please, call me Allesa. And yes, I do have a vacancy," she said with a coy smile. "Up the stairs, to the right, last door on your right. Breakfast is at seven o'clock."

As he picked up his knapsack and headed up the stairs, Allesa noticed his limp. "Can I get something for your leg?"

"No, I'm fine, but thanks," he replied.

His weariness prevailed over the discomfort in his leg. He drifted off to sleep quickly. Few dreams chased him this night. No shadows, just rest.

If not for the school bell's piercing ring outside his window, he would have slept through the morning. He sat up and moved to the edge of the bed where he noticed steam rising from a basin on the nightstand. A jar of ointment and a few fresh bandages were next to the basin. He smiled, remembering his refusal of help the night before. He gratefully, yet painfully, cleaned the wound and applied the ointment and bandages. He was a quick healer and knew he would soon be back to normal.

Anticipating the length of the journey ahead of him, he hastily dressed and packed his knapsack. Nothing was going to slow him down now, not even pain.

"Can I get you coffee?" asked Allesa, as he sat down at the last available table. "Please."

"Eggs and toast?"

Fritz enthusiastically replied, "Yes!" He had not had much to eat since leaving the kind elderly couple who had graciously taken him into their home earlier on his trek. The warmth of their words still echoed in his head. Fritz knew he would get it right. Besides, here he was, on his journey! He could smell the . . .

"Here you are," Allesa said, placing the plate of warm food on the table.

"Oh, thank you," he said, looking into her eyes. "By the way, thank you for the ointment and bandages. How did you know?"

"Oh, I am familiar with such a wound," she said. Seeing his knapsack was ready for travel, she sat down at his table and pointedly asked, "Where are you going?"

"I am headed to Dimen Castle."

"Dimen Castle! What a journey you have ahead of you!"

"Is it far?"

"Listen," said Allesa, "It can take longer than you think, but I am sure it will be a good pilgrimage."

"A good pilgrimage?"

"Yes."

"You've been there?" Fritz was intrigued to meet someone who knew his destination personally. "Tell me about the castle. Is the lord of the castle friendly? Is the castle as spectacular as they say it is?"

"The castle is quite spectacular, and its lord is an amazing man. But it is the journey that will be the most rewarding," Allesa said with a faint smile.

"The journey will be that enjoyable?"

"Oh, do not misunderstand me. I am not saying it will be easy. I am saying it will be rewarding."

"Do you think I will get to meet the lord of the castle?"

"Oh, yes, you will meet him." After a short pause, Allesa said, "Listen . . ."

Fritz cut her off mid-sentence, "By the way, I wanted to ask about the name of the inn. Why Listen Inn?"

Sighing, she said, "I will tell you, but you will have to listen to my explanation."

"I'm listening," he replied, stuffing his mouth with toast.

"The name reveals, first of all, that to understand, one must listen to hear the meaning. Secondly, it admonishes all who enter its doors, to listen, always listen. To understand, one must first listen."

"Understand what?"

"You, my friend, are not listening."

Fritz, looking offended, retorted, "Yes, I am."

"Yes," she replied, "with your physical ears, but not with your inner ears. If you were, you would hear it."

"Hear what?"

"Precisely," she said. "If you were truly listening, you would hear many things. All things speak! The rocks you climbed over to get here, speak boldly! The waters echo their voice. The plants you nonchalantly stepped on, sing! The animals you sent running for shelter as you stumbled through the woods, speak, and, surely, hear far more than you ever will!"

"I *want* to hear," Fritz said sincerely.

"Well, that's a start," said Allesa. "You must find a quiet place."

"I have been in many quiet places, and still haven't heard the things of which you speak," reflected Fritz.

"Then," said she, "there is one quiet place you obviously do not visit."

"Where?"

"Inside," she softly murmured.

"Inside what?"

"Inside yourself!"

Fritz put down his coffee, as puzzled as he was when face to face with the inscription on the rock. Allesa continued, "When you are finally able to quiet the noise within, quiet your thoughts, and quiet your needs, then you will hear."

He stood and reached for his knapsack. "Thank you for the lodging and the breakfast." Leaving a tip on the table, he excused himself, and headed toward the door. In the doorway, he turned and said, "I will try. To listen, that is."

She nodded and said, "Then you already are."

He smiled as he passed the fresh fruit and flower stands in the open market, and paused, straining to hear something audible coming from a table of neatly stacked apples. *Oh well*, he thought, ruefully.

At the edge of the village, he encountered the Elder who tended the sheep. "Pardon me, sir," said Fritz, "Do you know the way to Dimen Castle?"

"Of course I do," said the Elder. Face to the ground again, he raised his right arm and pointed north. His skin caught the morning sun and reflected jagged light off a roughly sealed wound.

Fritz, seeing the scarred arm, couldn't help interjecting, "How did you injure your arm, sir?"

The Elder eased his arm back inside his cloak, raised his head, looked Fritz in the eyes, and said, "Never mind that. Go down to the river and follow its edge. The water will eventually turn away from the road. When you come to the fork in the road, turn toward Isnot. There will be signs. Once you make it to Isnot, they will direct you to Dimen Castle."

"How long of a journey is it?"

"It depends," said the Elder.

"Depends on what?"

"If you get in a hurry, and are not paying close attention to the signs, it will take a long time. A very long time. But, if you carefully watch your walk, you will do well.

"Oh, one more thing," said the Elder. "Avoid going to Is. The people from Is always lie, but the people from Isnot always tell the truth."

Strange, thought Fritz. *Strange, indeed.* Why could he not get a straight answer from the Elder? How could a journey of a fixed length take one person a very long time and another less? Traversing a fixed path always takes less time if the traveler moves with haste. After all, the Elder did say the road was marked with signs. He was confident of his skills as a navigator, and quickly dismissed the warnings. Winter was coming, and he wanted to be back home by the first snowfall.

The road was level and smooth, meandering along the river's bank. The sound of water rippling around and over the rocks reminded him of Allesa's words. Were there voices he had missed on the first leg of his journey, voices that spoke, but whose sound fell on deaf ears? Surely he wasn't deaf, at least, not completely. She did say he could find these inner places, places where the sounds, the voices, and the echoes could be heard. It was a journey unlike any he had ever considered taking.

Why not? Why not make it two journeys in one? The thought had never crossed his mind before. His first intent, to make it to Dimen Castle and back before the first snowfall, was reasonable, and would not necessarily be hindered by a secondary venture. He could move quickly, and learn to listen to unfamiliar sounds along the way. It might even be entertaining and lighten the journey.

With his purpose intact, he tried to listen as he walked. It was an awkward challenge. He couldn't get his mind off Allesa's words. She kept referring to the noise, *the noise within*. How could he distinguish the difference between *the noise* and the sounds he needed to hear, *the voices*?

Fritz was so busy addressing these tough questions that he failed to notice he was walking in tall, dry grass. Where had the path gone? Where had his attention gone? Quickly turning around, he retraced his steps to the path. He remembered the Elder who warned of such digressions.   Fritz would not discard such advice so quickly again. But the words of the two, Allesa *and* the Elder, were both good words; yet, in tension.   One encouraged *listening*; and the other, *observation* of the signs to come. *Careful attention to the external, yet quiet within? Is that even possible?*

IsNot

Time floated by as the river turned away from the path's edge. All was well. It was just as the Elder had said. All the signs, so far, were very clear. For Fritz, there was a certain amount of comfort that crept in, comfort in knowing his gifts so well, comfort in having listened to the call to *listen*, and then, in turn, having listened so well to the Elder.

The trees that had beautifully lined the river's bank were disappearing behind him now. So, too, were the small river rocks that had covered the path. The path was now packed dirt, worn to a fine dust from many travelers. Surrounding the way were small cedars and briars. This was not, certainly, the most pleasant of trails to follow. Gradually, the flat land began to rise around the path. Soon the meadows were no more. In their place, hillsides turned into foothills. The path became a narrow valley and what lay beyond was now out of sight.

The path began to twist and turn, following the slopes of the surrounding hills. Fritz began to wonder if he would ever arrive at the fork in the road. This fear was mixed with thoughts of Allesa and the Elder. They were strange, but seemingly full of wisdom. As he pondered the two, he rounded another turn and saw the fork. It was unmistakable, thanks to the Elder's description. At that moment, a cold wind descended the hill that rose between the splitting trails and hit him head on, sending chills down his spine. Winter was closer than he had realized. But that was not the only thing troubling him now.

He stood gazing left, then right. There were no signs. There was no indication which way he should turn to head toward Isnot. Neither could he see beyond the hills. He was trapped; trapped by indecision; trapped by the knowledge that he could go the wrong way and never make it to Dimen Castle before winter.

The Elder had seemed so trustworthy, but perhaps Fritz's trust had been misplaced. Then again, maybe the signs were recently blown away. However, the wind descending the hill in front of him would have blown the signs back onto the path he had just traversed. There had been no such debris.

He felt colder in the midst of his confusion and indecision as the wind blew around his head and whistled in his ears. "What do I do now?" he asked himself as he pulled a scarf from his knapsack and wrapped it around his neck. He had come too far to turn back.

The whistling got louder, becoming too regular to be just the wind. It had rhythm. Suddenly he realized he would soon not be alone, for the whistling of the wind was mixed with the tonal whistling of someone coming around the bend of one of the forked paths. The echoes were too confusing to tell from which direction the whistling came. He waited, preparing to meet whomever it was from whichever trail they appeared.

The man was startled as he rounded the curve and saw Fritz. "Why do you stand here at this junction?" asked the whistler.

"I was told there would be signs to direct me to Isnot, but I have found none," explained Fritz, "Do you know the way to Isnot?"

"Why of course! I am from Isnot. Know it well! Just follow me," said the whistler.

Relieved, Fritz picked up the knapsack he had set down to rest his shoulders, ready to resume his journey. His nerves, however, were a bit unsettled. Perhaps, he was just recouping from the worry of not making it to Isnot in good time; perhaps, it was the cold settling into his bones; or, . . .

His thoughts suddenly shifted back to the Elder's words, "The people from Is always lie, but the people from Isnot always tell the truth." Clearly, the whistler was coming from one or the other of the two towns. Perhaps the Elder was wrong. He had been wrong about the signs. Surely, he could trust this whistling man!

Doubt, however, filled his mind. What if the whistler was from Is? If so, he would direct him away from Isnot, being a constant liar. But if he was from Isnot, incapable of telling a lie, he would direct him to Isnot. *How shall I tell one from the other, an Isian from an Isnotian?*

At that moment, he heard a voice from within saying, "*Listen. Listen.*" It was Allesa, or at least her words. He set his knapsack down and closed his eyes.

"Well, aren't you coming?" shouted the whistler.

"Just a moment," called Fritz, trying desperately to listen to whatever he was supposed to hear.

Moments passed and the whistler was growing impatient. Suddenly, a thought entered Fritz's mind. "That's it!" he cried.

"What's it?" asked the whistler.

Fritz looked into the face of the whistler and asked, "Which way would you go to get to your home town?"

"Why do you ask such a foolish question?" retorted the whistler.

"Answer my question!" yelled Fritz.

"OK, OK. There is no need to get all riled up. I will tell you. You would have to take the path I just came from."

"Thank you!" cried Fritz, as he picked up his knapsack and took off down the right hand side of the fork, down the path the whistler had just come from.

"Wait, don't you want to go to Isnot?"

"I do indeed," said Fritz. "And furthermore you are headed home to Is!"

"And just how have you come to know that?"

"You see," said Fritz, "If you had been from Isnot, you would have directed me down the path toward Isnot, since you would be unable to tell a lie. If, however, you were from Is, you would have directed me away from your home town, down the path to Isnot, since you would not be able to tell the truth. I now know the way to Isnot."

"Yes, but how do you know where I am from?"

"If you had been from Isnot you would not have said, 'Wait, don't you want to go to Isnot?'"

The whistler turned and continued down the path to Is, his whistling gradually fading into the wind. Fritz was so thankful that he had heard the voice within. Now he understood, at least in part. The voice within probably spoke more often than he heard.

Picking up the pace, he headed toward Isnot with a new peace. He was mistaken to have doubted the Elder. There *were* signs along the way. The whistler was one of them. His tread lightened as he thankfully replayed the Elder's words, determined not to question his wisdom again.

The terrain, however, quickly turned mountainous. Fritz marched onward, focused on making it over the pass to Isnot in good time. Switchbacks aided his climb through the thinning air.

Near the top, Fritz could see signs of winter. Several inches of snow had already fallen. The thin air and the slippery drag of the snow impeded his gait. His resolve to make it to Isnot, however, was unwavering.

Isnot. *What a peculiar name! The town of Isnot surely is! Why then is it called Isnot?* As he approached the wide ironclad gates, he noticed they were locked. "How is one to get in to such a town?" muttered Fritz with a crinkled brow.

"Hey, you!" cried a voice from somewhere. "That is not the way to get in to Isnot." Fritz looked up to see the head of a child hanging out of a window in the wall. "Go around to the small door on the side wall."

"And who are you?" asked Fritz.

"I am Fremd," said the high voice. "Go around to the side door, and I will let you in."

The door creaked as it opened. "It has been a while since we had a visitor here," said Fremd.

Fritz, puzzling over the comment, said, "I would think many travelers would find their way to Isnot."

"Oh, many try, but get lost in the journey. Isnot is not as easy to get to as you may think. You should know that. After all, it was a close call for you too, Fritz."

It took Fritz a second or two to absorb the words. "Wait a minute," replied Fritz, "How did you know I almost didn't make it here? How did you know I was even coming?" Then it dawned on Fritz that he hadn't even introduced himself; yet, Fremd knew his name.

Before Fritz had a chance to push the point any further, Fremd quickly shut the door and hurried off down the street. "Wait," cried Fritz.

"Well, come on then," yelled Fremd.

"Where are we going?"

"Nowhere in particular. I just wanted to see if you would follow me."

"Wait a minute," trembled Fritz as both parties came to a stop. "I need to understand what is going on here. Why should I follow you without knowing where we are going?"

"Do you trust me?" asked Fremd.

"I don't know you," replied Fritz.

"Then why are you following me? It seems to me that I should be the one asking the questions!" smirked Fremd.

"I am confused," said Fritz.

"No kidding!"

"Seriously!" pleaded Fritz, "The only face I have seen is that of a child. I was brought in through a small side door. I was asked to follow someone I don't know to somewhere I know not. Isnot is not what I expected."

"Precisely!" said Fremd.

"Precisely what?"

"Look," sighed Fremd "Do you or do you *not* want to make it to Dimen Castle?"

"Of course I . . . Wait a minute! You knew I had a close call getting here. You knew my name without an introduction. You know I am headed to Dimen Castle. How?"

"Perhaps a good night's sleep and a new tomorrow will help it make more sense," said Fremd, softly. "Come, I will show you to your room."

Fremd led Fritz down a narrow walkway to a little inn. Fritz had to duck his head to enter the door. Fremd called into the dim entryway, "Ratsel, our guest is here! Take him to his room. Make sure he has plenty of blankets and firewood. I will check on him in the morning."

Ratsel, an old man, hunched over from a curved spine, led Fritz to a very small room, with a door even smaller than the front door. Fritz ducked his head again, turned sideways, and narrowly entered the room. "Fresh linens are on the bed. There are plenty of blankets in the closet. The washroom is down the hall to the right. Ring the bell by the bed if you need anything."

"Thank you," replied Fritz. "By the way," he continued, "why do you take orders from a child?"

"A child?" snickered Ratsel. "You sure don't know much about Isnot, do you?"

"Well, he is a child after all, and you are an elderly man. I was taught that the young were to treat the elderly with great respect, not with commands."

"Everything is not as it seems," replied Ratsel. "I can tell you have more to learn from Fremd than I do!" he continued.

"You? Learn from a child?" asked Fritz.

"Everything is not as it seems in Isnot," Ratsel muttered as he left the room. "Get some rest. Fremd will be back in the morning."

From under the cover of thick blankets on a tiny bed, Fritz watched the flickering flames in the fireplace. Many strange places he had encountered. This, however, was the strangest of all. Questions filled his head. How could Fremd have known of his encounter with the whistler? It was apparent that Fremd and Ratsel knew he was coming, but how? They even had a room prepared. It was as though they knew him well. The questions continued as he drifted off to sleep.

It was early dawn when Fritz woke to hear Fremd and Ratsel talking down the hallway. "Well, Ratsel, I have news!" exclaimed Fremd.

"Tell me, tell me," replied Ratsel.

"The snowfall last night tied the longest standing record!"

"That's good!"

"No," replied Fremd, "that's bad. It amounted to twenty-one inches on the pass and three here in Isnot. We, my friend, are snowbound."

"Oh that's bad."

"No," replied Fremd, "that's good. We have enough food in storage to last the winter."

"Oh, that's good."

"No," replied Fremd, "that's bad. There is one more of us now."

"Oh, that's bad."

"No," replied Fremd, "that's good. We will have more time to spend with Fritz."

"Oh, that's good."

"I sure hope so!" laughed Fremd.

Fritz emerged from his room wearing the bathrobe that had been hanging by his door. Having heard the tail end of the conversation, Fritz asked, "So, is it good or bad?"

"Yes," Fremd jovially responded. He and Ratsel broke into laughter.

"Do you always make it a habit of listening in on other people's conversations?" asked Ratsel, continuing to laugh.

"Look," Fritz said with a furrowed brow, "I have to make it Dimen Castle before snowfall. I don't have time for such nonsense. I was told you would be able to tell me how to get there."

"Sure, it's just over the next mountain, but . . ."

Fritz cut him off, "Then tell me. I am leaving as soon as I dress and eat breakfast." Ratsel's face defied his aged appearance. For a second, he looked just like a child fighting back the urge to divulge a secret.

"I am sorry, my friend," Fremd replied soberly. "This may come as good news. On the other hand, it may come as bad news. It all depends on how you look at it."

"What?" responded Fritz impatiently.

"You might want to sit down. You are not going anywhere today. For that matter, you will not be going anywhere for the next several months," explained Fremd.

"Oh, yes, I will. I have a mission to fulfill. I want to fulfill it and be home before the first snowfall."

"Well, that is just the problem. You see, it snowed last night. And not just a little snow."

"How much?" asked Fritz.

"Twenty-one inches on the pass!"

"Twenty one inches!" yelled Fritz.

"Yes," interjected Ratsel, "And three here! Isn't it wonderful?!"

Fritz stared out the window, confounded. He was snowbound. Winter had arrived, and more snow would come. Months would pass before the winter snowfall would melt and permit passage over the mountain to Dimen Castle. No turning back either, they were locked in from all sides.

At noon, Ratsel called Fremd and Fritz to lunch. "What's for lunch today, Ratsel?" asked Fremd.

"Today we are having snow pea soup and humble pie."

"What's humble pie?" asked Fritz.

"You will find out soon enough!" replied Ratsel.

They sat down together. Fremd was served a very small bowl of soup and a tiny piece of pie. Fritz was served medium portions of both. Ratsel gave himself the largest portions of all. "Here in Isnot," commented Fremd, "the oldest gets more than he can eat and the youngest less than he needs." This seemed apparent to Fritz as he surveyed the servings.

Fritz finished his soup, slid his bowl aside, and took a bite of pie. He instantly coughed and sputtered, trying, bitterly, to swallow the bite of pie. "What is this?"

"It is clear that you are not ready for such a delicacy, Fritz. The time will come, however, when it will be the best thing you have ever tasted," promised Fremd.

Strange, indeed. Fritz noticed that Ratsel's bowl was empty and his pie gone. Fremd's food, on the other hand, was only partially eaten. "You told me that the eldest got more than he could eat and the youngest less than he needed. How then do you explain that Ratsel's portions are gone and yours are unfinished?" Fremd looked at Ratsel, then back at Fritz.

"Well, I guess it is time you learn more about Isnot. Come, let's go for a walk."

Fremd and Fritz bundled up for a walk in the freshly fallen snow. "Let's take the path around the town wall," Fremd said, cheerfully. Walking through the snow was easier than Fritz had expected. Dry and powdery snow did not cling heavily to boots.

They headed down the walkway towards the small door through which Fritz had entered. Turning left at the wall they began a stroll on the walkway that looped the town's interior. The wall to the right was tightly constructed with finely chiseled granite blocks, keeping light and wind from sneaking through its joints. To the left was an array of buildings, apparently constructed by the same mason that built the wall.

Fremd broke into a monologue. "In Isnot, the thing you expect the most is not. The thing that is not expected at all is. Large is small, and small is large. Old is young, and young is old. The past is not strange to us. Neither is the future. Sometimes the present is strange, but that is another issue. You see, Fritz, I am the oldest person in Isnot. Ratsel, on the other hand, is the youngest. Age and size, here in Isnot, are the inverse of what is known to the outside world."

"That explains Ratsel's behavior!" exclaimed Fritz.

"I beg your pardon," replied Fremd.

"Please do not take offense," Fritz continued, "but I have noticed Ratsel's childlike behavior on several occasions. I also wondered why he took orders from you. It is all adding up. And you, Fremd, wanted to see if I would follow you. No child wants to test a strange adult to see if they will follow them."

As they continued down the path, things strangely began to change. The town wall became disjointed. The buildings were much closer to each other. Some were even joined by the masonry. Puzzlement began to set in. Suddenly, Fritz realized where they were. Just ahead on the *left* was the small door he had entered when he first arrived. "Come on, Fritz, let's head back in and get something warm to drink," invited Fremd.

"But we were walking around the interior of the town. How did we end up out here?" Fritz looked back down the walkway behind them, but the curve of the wall blocked his view.

Fremd smiled, opened the door, and said, "Isnot is not without surprises!"

That evening, Fritz pondered the strangeness of Isnot as he peered out the window watching the snow fall. He would make the best of his stay here, trying to accept the strange character of Isnot as it was.

Days turned into weeks, and weeks into months. He had long given up his goal of trekking to Dimen Castle and back home within a couple of weeks. Somehow the goal seemed less important now. He would go to Dimen Castle, but not in such a rush. He was learning to accept the small, but strangely large, things in life. His large and noble goals were becoming insignificant. The enforced slow-down had its benefits.

Questions still remained. Yet, in the midst of such unknowns, a strange softening was happening. He was changing within. The strangest of all was his discovery that the pie was no longer bitter.

When the news came that the mountain pass was clear for passage, a tinge of sadness overcame Fritz. His new friends would remain in Isnot. He would go on. But the travels to come would be different. He would face them with a better understanding of life and of himself. He would try to carry the principles of Isnot with him beyond the mountain. Even if the outside world was not inverted like Isnot, he would carry some of its strangeness within.

"It is time to go," Fritz said sadly to Fremd and Ratsel. "What do I owe you for all your hospitality?"

Fremd walked up to Fritz, reached up, put his hand on his shoulder, and said, "You owe me an amount that you cannot count."

"Oh, I don't have much to give," replied Fritz.

"Well, there are two amounts that you cannot count. One is infinite. The other is nothing. I will settle for nothing," smiled Fremd.

Fritz hugged his friends and headed toward the small door he had come in through just months before. "Fritz, you cannot get out that way," called Fremd. "You can only enter by that door."

"But I thought . . ."

"Follow me," Fremd said, softly. Together they walked to the large iron clad gates. They opened easily with Fremd's gentle touch. "Take the northeast road over the mountain. When you are half way down the other side of the mountain, the road will fork. Stay on the northeast branch. It will lead you directly to Dimen Castle. Safe travels, my friend. Do watch your step. The road can be quite rocky."

As Fritz began the mountainous climb, he realized he was not limping. "My leg is not hurting!" he exclaimed to the trees and the melting snow. "But of course, that is what happens in Isnot!" His leg had completely healed during the months he was confined in Isnot; so had his misgivings about the delay. He traveled with the awareness that having been snowbound with his friends in Isnot was *not* coincidental. He was changed. "Life *is not* the same!" The words echoed off the surrounding slopes.

Dimen Castle

Previously, the two mountainous climbs had been among deciduous trees, mostly maples and oaks. On this northwestern range, however, the leafless silhouettes were dwindling. In their place, conifers were appearing in increasing height and density the further up the mountain he climbed. The little snow that remained was rapidly melting, filling the nearby streams with milky water. Signs of spring labored to push through the ground cover. Fresh, cool air filled his lungs with each intake of breath.

At the ridge, Fritz stopped to view the countless mountains undulating in waves ahead of him. They were very alive, yet frozen in time. He stood, dwelling on the naïve objective that had dictated his reactions and impatience at the start of his journey. Over the months, he had softened considerably.

Why not slow down and enjoy the moment? A bit surprised at himself for harboring such a spontaneous thought, he set his knapsack down and began to look about for firewood. The crackle of the cones and needles under his feet was warm and welcoming. He would use them for kindling and bedding.

The sky grew dark and yielded a display of stars unlike any he had ever seen. He lay back on his bed of needles and pulled his arms inside his woolen vest. The starlight was unhampered by the flickering flames. Placing another piece of wood on the fire, he marveled at the setting and at the peace he felt. *There is so much beyond this small rock we call home,* he thought as he gazed at a densely packed night sky and let his mind slide into quiet sleep.

Morning came quickly. The air was cold and the fire was gone. He roused himself with a few shivers and ate the bread and dried fruit Fremd had sent with him. He would warm himself with the hike to come rather than rekindle the fire.

The timber made it difficult to see how far down the mountainside he had gone. Rounding a lengthy switchback, he saw the split in the path. One fork headed northwest and the other proceeded northeast. Remembering Fremd's gentle words, he smiled as he took the northeast fork and continued the descent.

The steep trail gradually leveled out, leading Fritz into a pasture with grazing sheep. A boy sat perched on a boulder, staff in hand, watching the sheep. "Good day!" Fritz said, startling the boy.

"Good day, sir!" the boy replied.

"I was told this path would take me directly to Dimen Castle. How far is it from here?"

"Why it is right there, sir!" said the boy, pointing toward the opposite end of the long meadow.

"I see nothing," said Fritz.

"I didn't say you could see it, sir. I simply said it is there."

Fritz paused and began to replay the strangeness of Isnot. His insistence that things illogical were always illogical had been softened by the humbling inverse lessons from Fremd. The strangeness of Isnot, however, was very visible. Either this little shepherd was playing games with him or the limits of strangeness were being pushed even further.

"What do I have to do to see it?" Fritz asked, knowing the answer was likely to be as convoluted as any he had received yet.

"Take the path to the end of the meadow, turn left and you will see it," explained the boy. Somewhat exasperated, yet open to the possibility of another strange surprise, Fritz left the boy to tend his sheep and continued the path through the meadow.

The serene alpine view that Fritz had admired was disturbed as he looked up to the left, and noticed that one of the mountainsides was scorched. Green timbers were replaced with charred stumps. Snapped off at their bases, logs lay on their sides, as though prostrate before a king. *How could such a disaster have happened? How was it put out before it consumed the rest of the mountain and the lowland?*

Looking ahead once again, he could see that the path ended abruptly in front of a boulder. Still, no castle was in sight. *I can't believe I let that boy . . .* His thoughts reverted to Fremd's words, "It will lead you directly to Dimen Castle." He knew Fremd to be trustworthy; strange, but trustworthy.

Fritz had little option but to continue forward until he could touch the surface of the boulder, worn smooth by glaciers, wind and rain. With his right hand still rubbing the rock, he turned his head to the left. His heart leapt from his chest as he realized the castle wall was only yards away. Convinced he was hallucinating, he turned around and headed back down the meadow path. After a few yards, he turned about. He scanned the landscape carefully, but there was no structure to behold. He repeated his approach, turning left occasionally to test his sanity. *No castle. No castle.* As he approached the boulder, he turned to the left once more. *Castle! How can this be?*

From the distant end of the meadow, he heard the boy yell, "Do you see it now?" Too nervous to respond, he walked toward the castle wall. It towered above the lowly meadow. Gazing up, he tried to estimate its height. He could barely reach the top of the first layer of the stone foundation.

Hoping to find an entrance, he walked along the castle's wall. No entrance existed. He approached the corner of the wall and turned left, intending to search the adjacent wall. However, much to his dismay, the wall completely disappeared. Perplexed, he wandered back to the boulder and sat down, resting his head against the hard, smooth rock.

"Why do you sit there, young man?" Looking to the right, Fritz saw a man escorting the shepherd boy to the castle wall.

"I tried to find an entrance through the castle wall, but with no success. I am tired and hungry, so here I sit," Fritz said gruffly.

"Ah, a newcomer!" said the man as he and the boy passed by the boulder.

Fritz turned away, facing the meadow's end once more.

Suddenly, all was silent. Turning toward the wall again, Fritz realized the man and the boy were gone. *Gone!* He shook his head, blinked his eyes, and began to think they had not been real. Had he been hallucinating? Either way, it was not a good ending to what had been a wonderful trip over the mountain. Fremd hadn't told him it would be so difficult to get into the castle.

"Well, are you coming or not?" Fritz turned to see the man standing next to the castle wall beckoning him with his hand.

"Where did you go? Where did you come from? How did you do that? Are you real?" Fritz sputtered in confusion.

"Yes, I am quite real," said the man in a kind tone. "Come. I will show you how to get through the castle wall."

Fritz picked up his things, and walked toward the man. "Turn away from the wall to the right. Take twelve side steps to the left, then turn left again. Do you understand?"

"I am not sure," replied Fritz.

"Here, take my hand, and do exactly what I do." The man took Fritz's hand and stood next to the wall. Facing down the length of the wall he said, "Here we go. Twelve steps to the left!" In a flash, Fritz was not sure where he was. It was not light. Neither was it dark. Matter and space swirled around him like an ethereal dream. "Now turn left."

Fritz turned to see the interior of the castle wall. Turning back to his guide he asked, "What just happened?"

The man chuckled and said, "Welcome to Dimen Castle."

"How did we just come through a solid stone wall?"

"Are you hungry? Come, we will talk over dinner." The man led Fritz down a path through an area that resembled a park more than what he expected the interior of a castle to look like. The wall they had passed through was not a part of the castle structure as such, but rather a surrounding guardian. The stone path wound through aged fruit trees and flower beds just beginning to show signs of spring.

The path opened into a courtyard in front of the castle. Curving stairs climbed upward to a landing in front of a pair of tall, bronze-plated doors. The sides of the castle were supported with buttresses whose bases almost reached the exterior walls. Stained glass windows filled the spaces between the buttresses. Fritz had hoped the castle would be a glorious sight, but what his eyes beheld far surpassed his wildest expectations.

"Come on, dinner is waiting," urged the man. They quickly climbed the stairs. Just as their feet hit the landing the bronze doors opened.

"Welcome to Dimen Castle," echoed a voice through a foyer where rays of colored light, shining through a stained glass dome above, bounced off the floor and onto the walls. "Dinner is ready and waiting," said the noble looking man who greeted the two of them.

Fritz, numb by the strange events and the unknown hosts who led him to dinner, walked in silence. They left the foyer via a hallway lined with tapestry. Distant voices, muffled by the fabric on the walls, could be heard but not understood. Turning into a doorway off of the hallway, they entered a dining room. One lengthy table filled the center of the room. Candles, lining the center of the table, were lit and flickering. Standing around the table were twenty or more people waiting patiently for their meal.

"Friends, our new guest has arrived. I think it is time for some introductions," said the noble who led the two into the dining room. Turning to Fritz, he exclaimed, "I am Ganz."

Fritz, still nervous and confused, replied, "I am Fritz, Fritz Streuner."

The man who had shown Fritz through the wall said, "Fritz, I am Sorge. Over there is my wife, and here is my son, whom you met in the meadow."

Ganz invited everyone to take their places. "You sit next to me, Fritz," said Ganz. Picking up a glass of wine, Ganz lifted it into the air and said, "To Lord Zeitlos, our kind and generous host!"

"Here, here!" They all replied in unison.

Sitting down, the conversation began. "What do you think of Dimen Castle thus far, Fritz?" Ganz asked cheerfully.

"It is beautiful. It is also quite a mystery. I have many questions."

"There will be time for those. Here comes the food."

The servers brought dishes with various entrees. They did not ask who wanted which entree; they simply set them down in front of each guest. A plate of broiled fish was placed in front of Fritz. Fritz, however, was not paying much attention to the dish in front of him. Instead, he was focused on the other guests with their dishes. Much to his astonishment, the other guests were rotating their plates a quarter turn, inspecting the entree, and then turning their plates again.

He glanced at Ganz's plate and gasped. What had been broiled fish, like his, was now a grilled sirloin steak. Looking around, he observed many new entrees. Some had become smoked ham, and others, skewered shrimp. With each turn, the entrée changed to something new. Some guests, apparently deciding to settle for a previous selection, rotated their plates backwards to find an entrée they had passed.

Without asking, Fritz began rotating his plate. Finally settling on lobster tail, he timidly began to eat. There were too many questions to know where to begin. "Enjoying your meal, Fritz?" said Ganz with a mouth full of steak.

"Yes, sir."

"Now, what were those questions you had?"

Fritz, not sure where to start, blurted out, "The castle wall; how is it that I could see it when next to it, but not from anywhere else? And the entry through the wall? Explain that!"

Ganz set down his fork and said, "Dimen Castle shares only two of the three spatial dimensions common to the rest of the world. It can only be seen when viewed from a perspective that looks directly into the plane of those two dimensions. As to the entry through the wall, the only way to get through such a wall is to face a direction parallel to the wall, causing the wall to disappear, then move sideways into its third dimension."

"Why sideways?"

"Did you try simply walking into the wall, Fritz? It is pretty hard. You have to face a direction in which it does not exist, and then move through it."

Staring down at his plate, Fritz continued the questions, "You referred to Lord Zeitlos as a host. Why is everyone here a guest? Doesn't anyone in this room live here? And where is Lord Zeitlos?"

"You sure have a lot of questions!" Ganz chuckled. "Not everyone here is a guest. Sorge and his family are the caretakers of the castle. The rest of us are guests. Some, including me, have been here numerous times and know what to expect when visiting. As to Lord Zeitlos, he is currently away on a trip and is not expected back for quite some time. I am sorry you missed him."

Fritz's thoughts went back to Allesa's assurance that he would meet Lord Zeitlos. She probably did not know he was traveling at present. He couldn't hold that against her. She had given him too many words of advice that had proven true to doubt her now.

"One more question, Ganz."

"Oh, trust me," interrupted Ganz, "there will be many more!"

"Probably so," replied Fritz. "What kind of plates are these?"

"Aren't they delightful? They are dimensional plates. Here in Dimen Castle, as you will continue to find out, many different and contrasting things are actually one and the same thing. Even some contradictory things are one."

"What do you mean contradictory things?"

"For instance, small things can be large and large things can be small. Just by rotating the object or yourself! Allow me to illustrate." He motioned for Fritz to stand. "Look around you and take in the view. Now, hang your head down, facing the floor, and turn one complete circle to the left."

When Fritz raised his head he gasped at the sight. The room and its contents, including the people, were twice their original size! Without giving it a thought he quickly hung his head and turned completely around to the right. "How can this be? This is illogical. No such changes take place in my home country."

"Well, you are not in your home country!" laughed Ganz. Continuing, he said, "Look, these things are unheard of even just outside the castle walls. This unique ability to have multiple and differing appearances depending on one's perspective is found only inside the walls of Dimen Castle. Oh," Ganz interrupted himself, "here comes dessert!" The servers placed empty plates in front of each guest.

"There is nothing on the plates," said Fritz.

"Oh, I failed to mention that the options for dessert include nothing!" Again, each guest began to rotate his or her plate to choose a desert. Fritz settled on a new favorite: humble pie.

At the close of dinner, Ganz said, "Come, I will show you to your room. We will explore the castle tomorrow."

As they left the dining room, Fritz was surprised to find that the hallway was no longer covered with tapestry. Instead, it was lined with portraits. Some of them looked aged with cracks in the varnish. Others appeared to be more recent renderings. Pointing to some of the older ones, Fritz asked, "Are these former lords of the castle?"

"Oh, no," Ganz replied with a deep voice, "They are all of Lord Zeitlos."

"But, they don't look at all like the same person!"

"Remember," said Ganz, "Here in Dimen Castle, many dissimilar things may actually be one and the same." Fritz crinkled his brow. At the end of the hallway he paused, staring at the last portrait. "What is it, Fritz?" It looked hauntingly familiar.

"Oh, it's probably nothing," replied Fritz.

In the morning, Fritz wandered about the castle while waiting for the call to breakfast. He experimented with the perspective phenomenon. Statues changed. Images in the stained glass windows mutated. He smiled at the changes, but he understood little.

After breakfast, Ganz took Fritz on a tour. They saw magnificent libraries, music parlors, and scores of sculptures. The tour ended in front of a strange, iridescent door. Fritz moved from side to side, observing its radiant colors. "What is behind this door?"

"This," Ganz said softly, "This is the inner sanctuary of Dimen Castle. It is unlike anything you have ever beheld. However, not all who approach it can enter."

"Who can enter?"

Pointing to an inscription above the door, Ganz read, "Only Humble Learned May Enter Here."

"That probably doesn't include me," sighed Fritz.

At that moment, the door opened. "Oh, but it does, Fritz. Come."

The passage through the doorway was much like the passage through the castle wall, but more radiant. Once through, Fritz stood staring in silence. Before him was a miniature of the surrounding mountains and Dimen Castle; but, it was not simply a model. Looking closely and carefully, Fritz could see the sheep grazing in the meadow. They were alive and moving. He could hear them calling. People in and around the miniature castle could be seen walking and heard talking. "Look, but do not touch," Ganz said emphatically.

The room smelled of smoke. Fritz could see the mountainside scarred by fire. Looking around the room, he saw more signs of fire. The ceiling was charred. Smoke damage muted the color of the stained glass windows. "What happened?"

"A traveler, much like you, lost control of a campfire on the mountainside during a very dry time of year. The mountain was quickly engulfed in flames.   A few families lived on that mountainside. They lost everything except their lives."

Fritz broke into a cold sweat. If not for the dampness of the forest floor, his campfire could have caused a similar storm of damage. "How did the people get out?"

There was a long, still pause before Ganz began to speak, "Lord Zeitlos ran with all his might up the main entrance, down the corridors, and into this sanctuary. Throwing off his robe, he reached down into the fire, picked up each of the stranded lives, and set them down inside the castle walls. Knowing that the fire would soon reach the castle itself, he suffocated it with his arm.

From the vantage point of the people in the castle courtyards, a large arm descended from the sky and squelched the fire. Cries, from the sky above, shook the castle walls. In spite of the pain, Lord Zeitlos continued until the fire was extinguished.

As Lord Zeitlos came out of the inner sanctuary, he fainted from the pain. Sorge arrived at the sanctuary door just in time to catch him. He carried Lord Zeitlos to his room and tended to his wounds.

His arm took years to heal. The scars, as I can attest, remain and are most profound."

"Which arm?" Fritz interrupted.

"It was his right arm. Why do you ask?"

Fritz sat down on a chest next to one of the sanctuary walls. His furrowed face gradually turned into a smile. "I knew I had seen that face before!"

"What face?"

"The last portrait in the hallway leading from the dining room. It was him!"

"Who?"

"The Elder who gave me directions to Listen Inn and to Isnot. It was him! Lord Zeitlos! Allesa knew I would meet him. She probably knew I already had."

Ganz, now puzzled, looked inquisitively at Fritz. Fritz continued, "I do not smile at the sacrificing pain and scars, Ganz. I smile because I *have* met Lord Zeitlos. That was a crucial part of my mission. I wanted to see the castle, and then meet him. Little did I know that I would meet him, and then see the castle. What a kind and wise man! He so graciously gave me what I needed. And humble! He did not proclaim his name. He did not draw attention to his scars. He kindly answered my questions and gave me advice."

Leaving the inner sanctuary, Fritz decided to go outside for a breath of fresh air. He exited the bronze doors and stood in silence on the landing. His eyes grew wide as he surveyed the area surrounding the courtyard. The barren fruit trees that he had walked by when he first entered Dimen Castle were green and laden with fruit. The flower beds that had shown signs of the coming spring were now full of blooming plants, many now past their prime.

He sensed the presence of the two who surrounded him at that moment, Ganz on his right, and Sorge on his left. "This," said Sorge, "is the last surprise of Dimen Castle."

"I don't get it. I have been here for only a day."

"Within the walls of Dimen Castle, one day is like two hundred and forty to the outside world," said Ganz.

"You see," continued Sorge, "the plants share the soil with the outside world. They know their time."

Ganz handed Fritz his knapsack, and said, "If you are hoping to make it home before the first snowfall, you'd better get going. I stocked your sack with food for the journey." Fritz, overwhelmed with the concept of such a time discrepancy, wasn't sure if he was disappointed or not. He did, in fact, want to make it home before the first snowfall, but that was last winter!

"After you go through the wall, pick up the southeast trail behind the boulder. You will have to cross two significant mountains, a northeast range and a southeast range," directed Ganz. "I suggest you stop between the two of them at Fract Village. It is not difficult to find and will be a restful break. Ask for Teile, he will take care of you and give you directions from there."

Fritz turned and hugged Sorge, and then Ganz. "Thank you. Thank you, both."

"Safe and pleasant travels to you, Fritz!" they both exclaimed.

"Don't forget, look to the left, and twelve steps to the right!" said Sorge.

Fritz picked a ripe apple as he walked past the trees toward the castle wall. What more could he have dreamt? His mission was fulfilled. In addition, his small view of the world had been profoundly stretched. *And, oh, the many wonderful new friends!* Most of all, an internal softening had taken place, a softening that left a very strange peace, an ever increasing peace.

"OK, here we go," he said to himself, as he turned to the left and began his journey back through the wall. He landed on one leg outside the castle wall, and looking around, confirmed that summer was over. Fritz glanced back at the castle wall, and softly spoke, "Perhaps, I will see you again." Picking up the southeast trail behind the boulder, he headed toward the mountain.

Fract Village

The morning sun outside of the castle was still low on the horizon in front of Fritz. He smiled as he realized that Ganz and Sorge somehow knew the right moment had come for him to leave the castle.

The cool air was filled with the aroma of conifer resin. Small birds moved quietly through the trees. The meadow was behind him now. The path quickly moved into the wood.

Conifers. Fritz stopped for a moment to look closely at their branches. He had never taken the time to notice their peculiar patterns; repeating patterns; branches within branches; stems within stems; lined with leaves that were comprised of even smaller parts. For some, the smallest visible part was a needle. For others, it was bundles of scale-like tentacles. Regardless of their unique structures, all had one thing in common: parts were connected to parts that were connected to parts that were connected to parts that were connected to a tree trunk. For that matter, the trunks too were connected - to the earth.

His thoughts wandered to his many new friends who also were connected by stems. They were parts, too, so to speak, connected by interwoven journeys. Every one of his new friends had played an important role in his venture and in his growing understanding and peace. He smiled at the familiar patterns his thoughts naturally chased as well, always seeking to understand what life was giving him.

The ascent through the sweet trees was interspersed with the sun's blinding rays filtering through the trees. Fritz turned his eyes toward the ground more than once. The sunlight's autumnal direction gave him assurance that he was on a southeastern trek.

By the time he reached the top of the mountain, the sun was high and the trees had thinned at a bluff. He scanned the mountainside and the valley below and saw a network of streams merging into larger streams, leading into rivers. This pattern was much like within the trees: branches and streams were both interconnected, stemming from a base source, and flowing outward in a repetitive cycle. *Philosophical wanderings!* He chuckled at himself and his mind, and headed down the mountainside.

One of the streams he had observed from the peak was now running along the right side of the path. Fritz set down his pack and knelt next to the stream's edge. Cupping his hands, he took a drink of the clear, cold water. Opening his sack, he pulled out the apple he had picked on the way out of Dimen Castle. Without realizing it, he started rotating it. He caught himself with a laugh. *I guess I'm not in Dimen Castle anymore.* He bit into the crisp apple. *Hmm, I wonder what it would be now if I had rotated it before passing through the wall.*

Fritz gathered his things and continued his descent. As he glanced to the left, he saw another stream heading his direction; soon, it would merge with the one he was following. The new stream also had a path on its left. He should have seen the dilemma coming. The path he was on ended abruptly where the two streams merged. The path that had been on the left of the other stream continued on the left of the merged streams. To continue the descent, he would have to cross the stream.

Stepping from stone to stone, he managed to cross the stream without soaking his boots and continued on the path. As he walked, he recalled the view of merging waterways from the mountain's peak. He stopped in his tracks as it occurred to him that he would have to cross numerous merging waterways before arriving at Fract Village. No doubt, they would be progressively wider and deeper, and perhaps, even treacherous. Fritz shook his head as he muttered, "Ganz didn't say it would be easy or dry! He simply said it would not be difficult to find!"

Teile was waiting at the village's edge when a wet and cold Fritz arrived. "So," said he, "You took a bath, did you?"

Fritz smiled, as best he could, and asked, "Are you Teile?"

"Yes, I am Teile. Welcome to Fract Village. Perhaps, it would be best if we got you some dry clothes and hot tea."

At the village center, there was one large building. In many ways, it resembled the buildings on the outskirts of the village. It was larger, but very similar. As they approached its entry, Fritz stopped to look at the exterior wall constructed of bricks. The construction, in and of itself, was not so unusual. The bricks, however, were unusual. They were miniatures of the building they comprised! Looking even more closely, Fritz could see that they, too, were made of bricks that were miniatures of the bricks that formed the central building. "Come along, Fritz. I don't want you getting ill in those wet clothes," called Teile over his shoulder.

They followed a long narrow hallway into a seven-sided foyer. Each of the seven walls had an opening to a hallway. The walls, hallways, and ceilings were lined with mirrors. The sight was disorienting. Teile chuckled at the confused Fritz and said, "It takes getting used to. Isn't it amazing how one, let alone two, can be many?" Pointing down one of the hallways, he continued, "Your room is down that hallway, first door on the left. There are dry clothes on the bed. Leave your wet belongings outside the door. We will take care of them."

As Fritz looked around, he could see thousands upon thousands of images reflected off the walls. Some grew smaller and more distant as his eyes roamed the walls. "Which hallway do I follow?"

"Actually, any of them will do. Meet me back here, and we will have tea."

The hot tea was a welcomed tonic. After a few sips, Fritz noticed the cup he held. "How does it hold tea?" asked Fritz as he examined its structure. The cup, quite like the building they were in, was constructed of smaller cups that were constructed of smaller cups that were constructed of smaller cups . . . There were many apparent holes!

"Perhaps, this will help," offered Teile, "Think about the smallest cup that comprises the cups that comprise, well, eventually this cup. If it is, indeed, the smallest cup, then it should be able to hold tea. Right?"

"I suppose so."

"Well, then, if it holds tea, then the cup it helps to comprise will hold tea by virtue of the smaller cups within it that do, in fact, hold tea!"

"OK," replied Fritz, trying to keep up with the thought pattern.

"Well, if you carry that logic to its fullest extent, you have a cup of tea! No guarantee that it's hot, however," laughed Teile. "Individual things in Fract Village are actually many. They are made of parts quite like the part they make."

"Why?" asked Fritz.

"Why? You ask why?" questioned Teile. "My friend, you have many lessons to learn, not only about Fract Village, but about life."

"I am listening," replied Fritz calmly.

"Well, then I see you have learned at least one. All of life is made of parts that are made of parts, and so on, and so forth. Even outside Fract Village, life is so," Teile continued.

"I have never seen such things outside Fract Village," retorted Fritz.

"Oh, but you have, you have. For instance, each tiny experience you have had on your journey this far has contributed to a larger experience, perhaps a leg of your journey. Each leg of your journey contributes to a larger experience, such as the whole journey itself. But, it does not stop there. Each journey contributes to a larger voyage, perhaps that of a lifetime. Do not think that this journey is it! The sole journey of a lifetime? No, it is but a part of a larger journey that is, in turn, but a part of another.

"Even parts that appear not to be connected may, in fact, be intertwined. The challenge is, my friend, to not assume that the life you hold, or a journey you take, is an isolated entity. It may, in fact, be but a part of a much larger entity that is part of a larger entity, and so on.

"The reverse is also true. For instance, think of the parts that make up your very own body! You are made of parts that are made of parts that are made of parts that are made of parts. While not all parts explicitly resemble each other, as they do here in Fract Village, they do, in fact, have many similarities. Do not close yourself off to the repeated mysteries that lie outside your walls or to the ones that lie within." Having said that, Teile excused himself to check on dinner.

Fritz sat in silent contemplation, occasionally glancing at the reflections on the walls. He had been given much to ponder. He could see and understand some of the parallels, like the patterns in the trees and streams, but many were too vague to grasp. Perhaps, his narrow ambitions had obscured a larger picture.

Teile returned pushing a cart with plates, utensils, and several entrees, "Dinner is served!" They gathered around a small table with two chairs next to one of the seven walls. The dinner plates were, well, consistent with the rest of Fract Village, as were the entrees.

"We have Repetitious Roast, Iterative Beets, Successive Salad and, my favorite, Apple, Apple, Apple, Apple, Apple, Apple Pie."

"I am not even going to ask," said Fritz.

"Good, let's eat."

Dinner was quite good and filling, and filling, and filling, and . . .

"I know just what you need now, Fritz. You need a good storytelling! It is a tradition of ours that each evening following dinner, the residents of Fract Village gather at the village square for storytelling. This evening, it will be the infamous Glatten, the smoothest storyteller ever heard." Not wanting to offend his host, Fritz pushed off his sleepiness and accepted the invitation.

Teile introduced Fritz to some of his friends as they took a seat toward the back of the crowd, "And now, fellow Fract Villagers, the infamous, the incessant, the ever-repeating Glatten!" The applause was ear-piercing.

"Shhh! He's starting!" whispered through the crowd.

Glatten's strong, soft voice began, "Once upon a time, there lived a glorious storyteller in the land of Fable. He gathered around himself all those who longed for such a gift and would become his apprentice storytellers. He told them of a storyteller who once told a story of an old man giving a lecture on storytelling. It was quite an interesting story. He spoke of the day when storytelling was a rare gift possessed only by those known as storytellers. Furthermore, any given storyteller was not, officially, known as a storyteller unless they knew who the storyteller was who taught the storyteller who taught the storyteller who taught the would-be-official storyteller to tell stories. Once it was determined that such a would-be storyteller was, indeed, an official storyteller, they were given permission to stand in the town square and tell the following story . . .

"Once upon a time, there lived a glorious storyteller in the land of Fable. He gathered around himself all those who longed for such a gift and would become his apprentice storytellers. He told them of a storyteller who once told a story of an old man giving a lecture on storytelling. It was quite an interesting story. He spoke of the day when storytelling was a rare gift possessed only by those known as storytellers. Furthermore, any given storyteller was not, officially, known as a storyteller unless they knew who the storyteller was who taught the storyteller who taught the storyteller who taught the would-be-official storyteller to tell stories. Once it was determined that such a would-be storyteller was, indeed, an official storyteller, they were given permission to stand in the town square and tell the following story . . .

By this time, Fritz could hardly keep his eyes open. "Perhaps, you are too tired for such storytelling," Teile said, considerately.

"Yes," replied Fritz, "I think I better get some rest for tomorrow's journey." At that, he said good night, and quietly left the square.

Upon entering the mirrored foyer, he realized he couldn't tell which of the seven hallways led to his room. Remembering that Teile had said, "Actually, any of them will do," Fritz made a random choice of a hallway, and entered the first door on the left. He found his clothes, boots, and knapsack, clean and dry, all neatly stacked at the foot of the bed. His knapsack had been restocked with food for the next day's journey.

During the night, Fritz's dreams were very strange. The longest and most unsettling was a dream about a dream about a dream about . . . Fritz lost count of how deeply the dream was imbedded.

He woke several times trying to clear his mind of the repetition. By morning, he had managed to get only a few hours of sleep uninterrupted by dreams of dreams.

Fritz finished dressing, threw his knapsack over his shoulder, and left the room. Standing in the center of the foyer, he pondered the seven hallways. Given that it did not matter which hallway he chose coming in, it probably did not matter which he chose going out.

Sure, enough! He exited the building right where he had first entered with Teile. Looking around, he wondered if Teile would show up to give him directions out of the village and over the next mountain.

"Are you looking for Teile?" A chorus of small voices came from behind him. He turned around to see seven identical boys. "Follow me, and I will take you to him," they said. At that, all seven boys left in seven different directions.

"Wait, which of you do I follow?"

"Me!" They all exclaimed.

From behind Fritz, came a familiar voice, "Good morning, Fritz." Teile smiled at the practical joke the septuplets were trying to pull on Fritz, "They often take advantage of their village's reputation to pull pranks on visitors. Come, let us have breakfast."

While sharing boiled eggs, toast, and tea, Teile began to explain to Fritz how to get over the next mountain. "I will lead you to the south edge of the village; from there, head south toward the mountain. You will come to forks in the path three times. Any choice will lead you up the mountain to the pass, for they all converge near the top. However, if you do not want to get soaked again, you must stay with the rightmost path. It will provide you with the only continuous path that does not cross water. Once you get to the pass, you will be able to see Seekers Bridge. Now hear this very clearly, for you may lose your life if you do not:

"The path descending the mountain is quite steep. For that reason, it is very important that you watch, carefully, at all times. As you approach the bridge, the path will take a slight turn to the right. At that precise point, you must stop and look, carefully, to the left. There is a little-known path, very narrow, and often obscured by brush. You must find it, and take it. Do not proceed down the path to the right. Many a life has done so, never to return."

"What is so dangerous about the main path?" asked Fritz.

"It is known for treacherous rock slides. The path is loose, and even the slightest disturbance can cause a rock slide that will, certainly, take you with it down into Satisfaction Gorge."

"I will watch for it."

"Fritz, do not be so casual about it. It is very deceiving. It looks like the path leads directly to the bridge. Be on careful watch."

At the edge of the village, Teile gave one final warning, "Please be careful. Please be careful. Please be careful. Satisfaction Gorge is full of skeletons."

"Thank you, Teile. I deeply appreciate your hospitality and concern."

"Farewell, friend," said Teile, and with that parting benediction, Fritz turned and headed south.

Reflective Cabin

The air was cold. Wind descended the mountainside causing Fritz to squint and pull his scarf close to his neck. The conifers had all but disappeared, giving way to grand oaks. Dry leaves barely clung to the branches. The wind moved freely through the trees, unlike within the sheltering conifers, but reminiscent of home.

The trek was slow. Fritz was tired from little sleep the night before. The thick air hampered his gait. His knapsack seemed heavier than usual. Perhaps a stop at the peak would refresh him before a cautious descent.

The sun was nowhere to be seen. Clouds, heavily laden with moisture, rolled across the sky; yet, the wood was a beautiful sight. Leaves partially covered the ground, and tree silhouettes outlined a very appealing path. The path was wide enough to be unmistakable, and smooth enough to walk without worry of stumbling.

The forks were just as Teile had said. Staying with the right-most fork each time, Fritz continued up the mountain without fording a waterway. His confidence in Teile's words grew, but so did his concern with the warnings.

Fritz set his knapsack down to take in the view from the mountaintop. The climb had taken him much longer than he had hoped. He took little time to eat what had been so kindly packed for him. Rest would have to wait. If the descent was truly as treacherous as Teile had warned, he would need to make up time where he could. There would be time for rest at home.

Just beyond the ridge, Fritz looked down at the gorge and could see the bridge that crossed its expanse. It was not at all what he had expected. It was a rope bridge. Even at such a distance, he could see that the wind moved through the gorge with force, tossing the bridge from side to side. Fear overcame his previous thoughts of comfort and home. He hadn't taken Teile seriously enough.

The northerly wind that had hindered his ascent now aided his descent. Even though it was bitter to his face, his knees thanked its support. His surefootedness was replaced with tentative steps amid loose rocks. Picking up a broken branch, he fashioned a walking stick for stability.

Going slowly, he began to consider the time of day. Even with an obscured sun, he knew it had to be getting on into the afternoon. His energy was torn between focusing on the difficult path and the warnings Teile had offered repeatedly.

He reached forward with his stick to catch himself when he tripped on a rock. The commotion sent a couple of rocks tumbling down the incline. Wondering if he had passed the cut off he had been warned to carefully watch for, his heart sank; yet, there had been no turn to the right. He gathered his thoughts and continued downward.

The bend in the path was more subtle than he had expected. He was sure it was the turn Teile had warned of after careful examination. There had been a glimpse of the bridge not long before. Scanning to the left, he saw no obvious path given the undergrowth amid the trees. Moving to the edge of the rocky trail, he looked for signs of previous travelers.

His thoughts drifted to Allesa's call to listen, Fremd's embrace of the strange, Ganz's comfort in a timeless castle, and Teile's repeated words. *What would they do at this moment?*

He scanned left, then right. Scanning left again, he stopped suddenly. Behind the undergrowth, and amid the trees, stood a deer. As quickly, and as quietly, as the deer had entered the wood before him, it took off through the autumn leaves, down and away.

Stepping through the brush and into the wood, he found an area of compact leaves where deer had been resting. Looking beyond, he saw a narrow path apparently worn by deer. He was not unfamiliar with the habits of deer. They make their own paths when necessary, but often use manmade paths to avoid scrapes with branches and undergrowth. Perhaps it was a path worth exploring. At least it was away from loose rock.

Ducking his head a few times to avoid low branches, he continued down the trail. It was narrow indeed. Occasionally scraping tree trunks as he went, he continued down and away from the main path.

The trail led him out onto a rocky ledge, right in front of the bridge. The deer trail turned and continued on along the gorge's edge. He smiled as he remembered Teile's concerned expression.

The smile soon gave way to the sight before him. He faced a swaying rope bridge, undulating with wind-driven waves. Looking down . . .

Suffice it to say, he quickly chose not to look down. He had faced numerous perplexing situations on his journey, but this was not perplexing. It was frightening. The only consoling factor in what he saw was that the ropes and slats were fairly new. They appeared strong and able to withstand the wind's torment. With that little bit of encouragement, he took a step onto the bridge.

Having left his walking stick behind, he gripped both ropes as tightly as possible. In spite of wanting to avoid looking down, he had to at least glance to avoid the spaces between the slats. On he went.

A dozen paces into the crossing, he lost his grip with one hand as the wind snapped at the ropes. Instinctively, he dropped low, avoiding being hurled over the rope's edge. Shaking profusely as he held his low posture, he considered returning; but in looking back, he realized that it would be as treacherous to return as it would be to keep going. Keeping his low profile and an even tighter grip, he continued.

Fritz collapsed on the opposite rocky ledge. He had crossed Seekers Bridge and had denied Satisfaction Gorge. Weak with tremors, he huddled among the rocks and rested his head.

Sleep came without warning. Fritz woke to a sky that had grown dark. Quickly slipping his arms through the straps of his knapsack, he turned to look for the trail. Climbing up from the rocky ledge, he discovered that the trail was level and smooth; but darkness was falling quickly, making it difficult to see the trail and its heading. *I can't stay here for the night. The wind is too strong and the chill is deep.*

He stopped and released a lengthy sigh. After a few moments of reflection, he resigned himself to a frigid night and slipped his knapsack off. Leaning against a tree, he remembered the starry night on the mountaintop before his descent to Dimen Castle. Tonight, however, no stars blessed his eyes and no fire warmed his soul. He stared off into the woods imagining a ray of hope.

Imagination. That's all it was. Or was it? He was too numb to know the difference. It was just a flicker. *It was a flicker!* Through the woods, Fritz could barely see a dim flickering light. His eyes grew wide with anticipation. He grabbed his sack and took off. Stumbling over downed trees and rocks, Fritz frantically ran on, determined to make it to the source of light.

All at once, it was gone. The light was gone. It couldn't have been his imagination. It was real. He saw it. *It was there!* Or was it?

Whether it had been real or imaginary, he decided to walk in the direction, or perceived direction, of what had been a ray of hope. His walk was now calm, unlike the stumbling scurry he had engaged in just moments before. He carefully felt his way with his hands and feet, hoping to avoid another stumble.

After a few near misses, he stopped to take in an old familiar smell that tugged at his resolve to keep going. It was burning wood. *Oh, what a warm smell.* He increased his pace a bit, aware of obstacles nonetheless.

He approached the cabin with a cautious hope. The smoke from the chimney gave him just cause to believe someone was home.

Giving little thought to the hazards of waking up its residents, Fritz put his cold knuckles to the door.

Inside, his knock was heard.

"Hoff, do you hear that?"

"Hear what?" No sooner were the words spoken than Hoff did hear the knocking.

"No one would be at our door this time of night without good cause. Not out here in the wood," said Liebe. Hoff rose to check.

"Who is it?"

"I am sorry, sir. I am cold and need a place to stay for the night." Hearing the voice through the locked door, Hoff decided to open it. In stumbled a cold and weary stranger.

Liebe, putting on her robe, exclaimed, "For heaven's sake, Hoff! He's cold, and probably hungry. I will make some tea." Hoff led the young man to a chair by the fireplace and draped a woolen blanket over his shoulders.

"Who are you, and what are you doing on Seekers Mountain in weather like this and at this time of night?" questioned Hoff.

"Hoff, give him a chance to warm up before badgering him with questions." Liebe handed a cup of hot tea to the frigid young man.

After a few sips of tea, Fritz turned to the couple and softly said, "Thank you." Hoff turned and looked at Liebe. Without another spoken word, they knew. Liebe rose to get some extra bedding. Together she and Hoff made a makeshift bed next to the fireplace.

"No need to talk now. There will be plenty of time for that in the morning. Get some sleep," Hoff said warmly.

It took only moments of staring at the fire for Fritz to fade into sleep, a very deep sleep. No dreams. No fears. No cold. Only warm restful slumber.

Hoff and Liebe moved quietly in the morning. Hoff carefully put more logs on the fire. Liebe put bacon on the stove. They smiled as they glanced at each other. They had helped many travelers in their years on Seeker Mountain. This was a young one.

The crackling smell roused Fritz. "Good morning!" Liebe said cheerfully.

"Good morning," replied Fritz.

"Breakfast will be ready in a few minutes. Perhaps you would like to freshen up? You may use the bathroom down the hall to the left."

Looking in the mirror, Fritz saw a dirty, weathered face. It had been a long journey, but now he was near the journey's end. *Very near.*

After cleaning up, he returned to the common room that combined a living room, a dining room, and a kitchen. The great room's high ceiling was supported with timbers. The fireplace was grand, made from large stones, probably gathered from the mountainside.

"Have a seat here." Hoff and Liebe brought breakfast plates to the table and sat down with him.

"Our names are Hoff and Liebe," said Hoff as he passed the bacon. "And you are?"

"My name is Fritz Streuner."

"How long have you been on your quest?"

"Quest?"

"Yes, your journey."

"Oh. It was going to be a short two-week visit to Dimen Castle, but it turned into a year-long trek. I am almost home. My journey will soon be over."

"Oh? Soon over?"

"Yes, I am ready to be done with my travels."

"You know," said Hoff, as he sat back in his chair, "we have met many a traveler who was on their way home. At least, so they thought. It is interesting how that can change."

"Not me, I accomplished what I set out to do, and now I am ready to go home."

Breakfast was restoring, not to mention incredibly delicious. Fritz helped clear the table, and walked over to the window to look out at the surroundings. The view was distorted. "You won't see much through that thick ice," Hoff said.

"Ice?"

"Why, yes. During the night, we had a massive ice storm. About two inches accumulated in this area," replied Hoff.

"But I need to leave. I want to get home before the first snowfall."

"It appears as though you will not be going anywhere for at least a few days. You are more than welcome to stay here with us."

Fritz continued to look through the ice at the distorted images. Trees appeared twisted. The mountain he had come across was in an upheaval. A squirrel moved across the deck railing, changing shape as it hopped. Hoff stood next to Fritz. "Isn't it interesting how the images are distorted?" After a pause, he continued, "Life can be that way, Fritz."

"What do you mean?"

"Sometimes, we are sure that we understand what we see. We think we see things as they really are. The problem is that life and its experiences cover our eyes with ice, as it were, distorting what we see."

"For instance?"

"Well, since you asked, how about your perception that your journey is almost over? Could that be a distorted image?" Fritz looked at him intently. Hoff gently continued, "I just ask you to consider the possibility."

Return

The next few days in the cabin with Hoff and Liebe were days of contemplation. There were, of course, very few other things to do. His hosts were very caring and thoughtful, allowing him plenty of time to sit in solitude next to the fireplace pondering his journey.

The ice slowly melted. By the third day, enough had melted to permit Hoff to open the door onto the deck. Fritz put on his vest and stepped out into fresh air. The view was gorgeous. The mountain glistened as rays of sunlight penetrated the remaining ice. The distortion was gone. He saw the mountain for what it was. The squirrel was back, attempting to dig food out of a frozen birdfeeder. As it ran across the rail, its body and tail flowed like undulating waves of water.

Melting. It had taken place outside, and inside. The ice over his eyes was slowly giving way, providing a clearer view of his journey, the inadequacy of a very small journey. What previously seemed prolonged, now seemed quite short. The journey he had intended to take was simple, not complex, and not difficult to understand. Instead, he had been pushed outside his comfort zones on many occasions and forced to let go of his shortsighted objectives. He had been challenged to consider possibilities previously out of the realm of, well, the realm of common sense. In exchange, the journey had proven rich, much richer than he had hoped; he was rich with new friends, and full of maturing tensions. He was not disappointed; rather, he felt a sense of strength and an odd expectancy.

Continuing the journey presented another dilemma. If he were to continue, what guarantee would preserve his new crisp images? What if they, too, were distorted by remaining ice? Would there be further melting? And, more melting after that? Where, and when, would it end?

"Hoff," Fritz asked over lunch, "how do you know when the melting is done?"

Hoff let out a gentle sigh and said, "That is an incredibly important question, Fritz, and one that is difficult to answer. Perhaps, you must continue the journey to find out!"

That evening after dinner, the three of them sat around the fireplace. The room was silent, but not empty. Glances of warmth, and a wealth of thoughts flowed through the spaces between them.

Finally, Fritz broke the silence, "I have to go back."

"Back where?" asked Liebe.

Fritz looked her in the eyes and said, "Back to Dimen Castle. I want to know more. I want to understand. There are so many questions. I need time with Lord Zeitlos. Perhaps, he will be there this time."

"Did you not see him on your previous journey?"

"Yes, but I did not know at the time who it was that gave me directions."

"Will you know him the next time you see him?"

"Of course. I know what he looks like now."

"Do you?" asked Liebe with wide-open eyes.

Instantly, Fritz's mind went back to the portraits in the hallway at Dimen Castle. They were very different portrayals of the same person; so different, that he had wrongly assumed they were previous lords. "How, then, shall I know when I see him?"

Liebe set her knitting on the hearth and leaned forward in her chair. "Be always on the watch. He appears when least expected. Look everyone in the eyes, pondering the possibilities. Never stop seeking him. Never stop seeking to understand. You know by now that he is not to be contained by Dimen Castle."

During the night, Fritz restlessly pondered Liebe's words. They were rich, yet disconcerting. He truly wanted to see Lord Zeitlos again. But, would he be quick enough to recognize those eyes? Would Lord Zeitlos be a hunched over old man again? What other forms does he assume? Why does he challenge a seeker so?

In the morning, Fritz found a warm breakfast waiting on the table, but only one place was set. Beside the teacup was a note:

> *Fritz, stay as long as you need. We are heading south*
> *for winter. If you decide to go back to Dimen Castle, you*
> *will need to go west over the mountain, then head north.*
> *Seekers Bridge went down during the ice storm. Wish you*
> *well.*

He walked over to the window and looked out over the mountains and Satisfaction Gorge. He was not satisfied. He could not go home. He would pack and leave for Dimen Castle after breakfast.

A few paces from the cabin, he turned and softly said, "Thank you. I hope we meet again, friends."

The air was cool, but the sun was warm to his skin. The slippery autumn leaves all but covered the ground. They made the climb a challenge, as they deceivingly obscured the rocky path.

As Fritz climbed, he thought of all the friends who had so graciously brushed some of his roughness away. How fortunate he was to have encountered such seasoned individuals!

Near the ridge, the rocky path that had demanded great attentiveness during the climb became smooth. The covering of leaves still made it a challenge to see. Autumn filled the air. Sunlight pierced the wood where it could, scattering light over the fallen leaves. The color was beautiful. It was almost as though . . .

"Uh!!!"

With his face in the leaves and dirt, and his shin thumping with pain he tried to gather his frazzled senses. He lifted his head, spit out the leafy dirt, and gazed back over his shoulder. If only he had been watching the path instead of the sunlight passing through the trees!

Rising slowly to his feet, he brushed off the debris and examined his leg. Blood ran down his shin. He pulled out a ragged kerchief and tied it around the wound. He consoled himself, knowing it would heal in time.

Looking up once again, he paid a glance to the obstacle that caused him injury. But the glance, without conscious effort, turned to fixation. It was just a rock. Or was it?

Perplexed, he knelt in the damp debris next to the rock. No simple geological fracture produced its sheer faces, for there were signs of artistic effort in its smooth facets and sharp edges. He brushed away the leaves and dirt to reveal an inscription that read,

Listen!

Is is not and IsNot is

Many are one

One is many

Seek to understand!

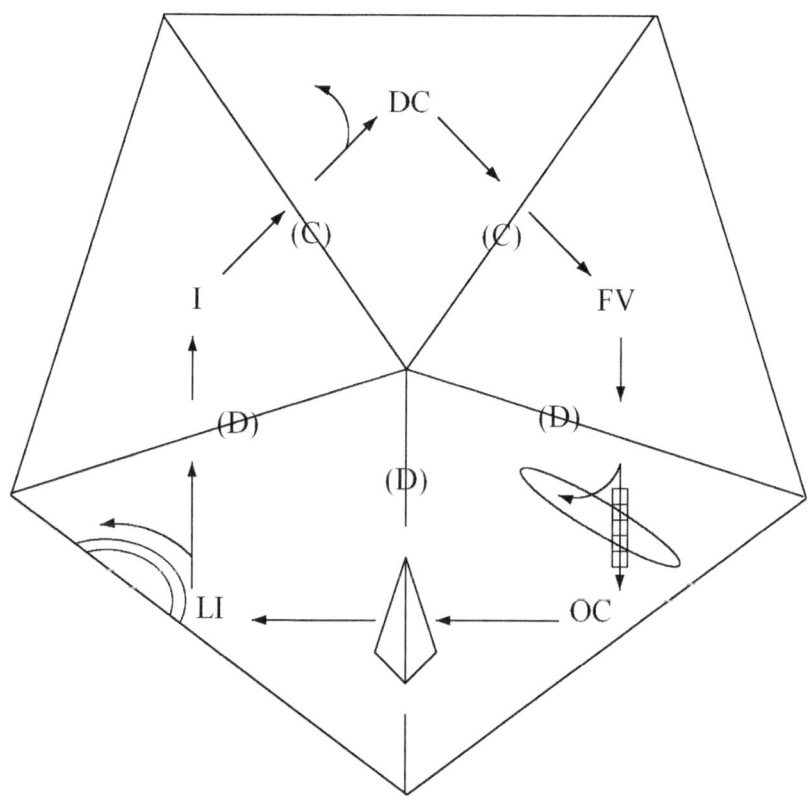

The Cast

Name	Translation
Fritz Streuner	Peaceful Wanderer
Allesa Horen	Everyone Listen!
Fremd	Strange
Ratsel	Riddle
Sorge	Caregiver
Ganz	Undivided
Zeitlos	Timeless
Teile	Component
Glatten	Smooth
Hoff	Hope
Liebe	Love

www.ingramcontent.com/pod-product-compliance
Lightning Source LLC
Chambersburg PA
CBHW071344130626
46556CB00005B/2028

*   9 7 8 0 6 9 2 9 3 8 9 5 9   *